"A goal without a plan is just a wish"

Antoine de Saint-Exupéry

SEAN GOES TO
BARCEL●NA

By

TANYA PREMINGER

Illustrations

ELETTRA CUDIGNOTTO

To Sean, my light and my inspiration.

Contents

TANYA PREMINGER

Do You Play Soccer?

Sean is leaning across the airplane tray table, concentrating on coloring his Barcelona Soccer Club book. He finishes coloring Messi's image and writes around it in red: "Messi is the king! Ronaldo does not compare! Ronaldo is an ego-maniac! Real Madrid is the worst soccer team ever. They play in a baby league, boo, boo, boo!"

He closes the book, satisfied, and looks out the airplane window, watching cottony clouds float in the bright blue sky. He turns to Mommy in the seat next to his.

"Mommy, when we get to Barcelona, you need to buy me a Barcelona scarf and a Barcelona shirt."

Mommy puts down the Barcelona city map she was studying and shakes her head.

"Why? You never wear a scarf, and you already have a Barca shirt."

"It's a soccer scarf! I can't go to the game without a scarf. And my Barca shirt is old. Barca has new uniforms now," Sean explains.

Mommy sighs.

"Buy me this, buy me that…Please, don't start with me, Sean. I bought you this whole trip. I think that's enough."

"Mommy, I will be sad if I don't have the scarf…" Sean makes an exaggerated pouty face.

"Fine, be sad," Mommy replies.

The cabin illuminates, a bell rings, and a deep male voice is heard over the PA system: "Ladies and gentlemen, we have started our descent to Barcelona International Airport. Please make sure your seatbelts are securely fastened and that all carry-on luggage is stowed underneath the seat in front of you. Thank you."

"Mommy, I cannot watch the game without a Barca scarf. Please!" whines Sean.

"Sean, we can't afford everything." Mommy pushes her map into her backpack.

"The scarf is not expensive," says Sean.

"It's not only the scarf. It's the plane tickets, the game tickets, the accommodations…" Mommy lists.

"But, Mommy, please!" Sean cries.

"Forget it, I said no," Mommy says with determination. "Fasten your seatbelt, please."

A flight attendant approaches them with a smile.

"You need to close your tray table now," she says to Sean. Then she notices his Barca uniform.

"You like soccer?" she asks.

Sean lowers his head timidly and does not answer.

"Sean...the lady just asked you something." Mommy nudges him gently.

Sean leans his cheek on his shoulder and stares at the floor. Mommy and the flight attendant look at each other, smiling, waiting.

"Sean...where are your manners? Why don't you answer?" Mommy whispers in his ear.

Sean keeps quiet and does not raise his eyes.

"He is shy around strangers," Mommy apologizes. "But yes, he LOVES soccer."

"Do you play soccer yourself?" The stewardess tries again, offering Sean a candy from the straw basket in her hand.

This time Sean looks at her, nods his head timidly, and takes a candy.

"He plays in a club," Mommy says proudly. "He practices three times a week. He wants to be like Messi, the famous football player."

"How cool! I love soccer, too," says the flight attendant. "Are you going to see a Barca game while in town?"

"Yes, we are. We are very excited about that," Mommy beams.

"Oh, you are so lucky!" the flight attendant tells Sean. "Mommy is taking you to a Barca game! It's an experience of a lifetime. Did you make sure to thank your mommy?"

Embarrassed, Sean hides his face in his airplane blanket.

The flight attendant laughs.

"Enjoy your stay in Barcelona!" she says as she continues making her way down the aisle.

Sean takes the blanket off his head and turns to Mommy.

"Mommy, you are the best mommy in the world."

"Thanks, Seany." Mommy smiles and kisses his forehead.

"You are the most kind, smart, amazing mommy ever!"

Mommy laughs happily.

"Please buy me the scarf, please!"

"Oh, stop it. I'm not buying the scarf," Mommy says firmly.

"Mommy, I love you so much!"

"Stop working me, Sean. I know what you're doing. Please put your shoes on."

Suddenly, the plane shakes violently.

"Oh, my gosh, turbulence!" cringes Mommy.

Sean pats her knee reassuringly.

"Sweet, sweet Mommy, you are the coolest mommy ever. Please, please buy me the scarf!"

The plane shakes again.

"We will see. Okay?" Mommy tightens their seatbelts and takes a deep breath.

4

Taxi Drive Down La Rambla

Sean runs a hand through his hair to check that his hairdo is in place and carefully drapes his brand-new Barca scarf around his neck. He looks out the cab window inquisitively.

The cab is driving along the famous La Rambla Avenue. The morning sun shines in between the leaves of the old trees, and shadows play on Sean's and Mommy's faces as they observe the crowd from the backseat of the taxi. Vendors, tourists, and locals overflow the walkways. The avenue is packed with cafes, restaurants, souvenir shops, kiosks, and flower stalls.

"I can't believe they have an official Barca shop in the airport right next to the baggage claim," groans Mommy.

"Don't worry about it, Mommy." Sean smiles contentedly. "Thanks again for my scarf!"

"What a tourist trap…" Mommy grumbles on.

"Will you get me the Barca shirt tomorrow?" Sean asks.

"No way!"

The taxi driver, a young man wearing colorful Indian garb, laughs. He turns down the Indian pop music playing on the radio.

"You like Barcelona soccer, ma'am?" he asks in a heavy accent.

"Yes, we love soccer. We are going to see Messi play!" exclaims Mommy.

"My son love the soccer," the driver says, glancing at them in the rearview mirror.

"So all the kids in Spain are crazy about soccer, too?" asks Mommy.

"Yes, yes." The driver grins.

They continue their drive, passing beautiful eighteenth-century buildings with ornamented windows and elaborate iron work on the balcony railings.

"You get Messi autograph?" the driver asks.

"Well…" smiles Mommy, "we will get it if we have the chance."

The cab turns onto a narrow alley in the Barcelona old quarter.

"How long time you stay Barcelona?" asks the driver.

"Five days," answers Mommy.

"No long."

"Yes, but we have many things to do. Today we are going to the Camp Nou museum," says Mommy cheerfully.

The taxi driver slows down and inspects the building numbers.

"This the address, ma'am?"

Mommy checks her notes. "Yes."

"Where the hotel?"

"Oh, it's not a hotel. It's an apartment."

"So we here." The driver hands them a business card. "My name is Arjun. My phone number here." He points at the number on the card. "I tour guide. I make good tours. I get you Messi autograph."

"Thanks so much, but we've got a lot planned as it is," says Mommy politely.

But the driver isn't quite ready to give up yet. "Not expensive!" he insists as he helps them with their luggage.

Mommy and Sean just smile at each other.

Tiki Taka

Sean, wearing his new Barca shirt and Barca scarf, stands in line next to Mommy at the entrance of the Camp Nou museum, fidgeting with excitement. People from all over the world, young and old, dressed in a variety of styles from all different cultures, wait patiently and chat excitedly in Spanish, English, French, German, Arabic, and Hebrew.

"Mommy, will I get Messi's autograph?" Sean asks.

"Sean, this is a museum. Messi is not here."

"So I won't see Messi?"

"Not here, at least."

"But, Mommy, I want to tell him I love him."

"Sean, he is a famous person. It won't be easy to meet him."

"But maybe he is coming to the stadium for a training?"

"I don't think Barca players train here," Mommy replies.

"So how will I get an autograph? Can we call Arjun the taxi driver?" Sean asks.

Mommy chuckles.

"I don't think he can arrange for us to meet Messi."

"Please, Mommy...I want to see Messi so much. You are the best, best mommy ever."

"Oh, Sean." Mommy laughs. "That tactic of yours is not going to work for you this time."

Finally, they buy their tickets, pass the entrance guard, and walk into a long corridor that leads to the Camp Nou stadium. Tall windows stretch along the walls, and glass frames with posters of the famous FC Barcelona players stand at equal intervals. All the visitors, Mommy and Sean included, pose next to each poster and take pictures.

In the first hall, floor-to-ceiling interactive screens display the FC Barcelona history from its inception in 1899. In a row of glass boxes, all the original trophies glow in the dark. A special area is dedicated to Messi's awards alone.

"Sean, look! The six trophies Barca won in 2009. It says here that no soccer club has ever achieved that before," Mommy points out.

"I know that, Mommy," Sean sneers. "You can't teach me anything about soccer."

"Oh, excuse me!" Mommy says and points at a long paragraph on the digital screen.

"Please read this to me," she asks.

"Read all that? It's too long," huffs Sean.

"So read half of it."

"Why do you want me to read it?"

"Because I want you to practice reading, and be smart, and know things."

"Forget it, Mommy, I'm not the type."

Mommy sighs.

"You don't know what type you are. You are only eight years old."

"I know that I'm going to be a soccer player," beams Sean.

Next, they visit the press conference room, where interviews are given to the press after games. They inspect the guest team locker rooms, with open showers, a big Jacuzzi in the center of the room, several massage tables, and a free drink machine that impresses Sean the most.

Soon enough, they arrive at the players' tunnel. FC Barcelona logos and flags are painted all over the walls. This is where the soccer players walk to the Camp Nou pitch. The PA system blasts out the sounds of a crowd cheering, and commentators announce the names of the Barcelona first team players: Messi, Neymar, Suarez. The visitors are thrilled and take zillions of pictures.

"Wow!" exclaims Sean as he stands in the same place he has seen so many times on TV.

"Stay close to me, please. I don't want you to get lost here," Mommy says to Sean.

"Don't worry, Mommy."

"Really? What will you do if you get lost?"

"I will not get lost."

Mommy is not satisfied with that.

"Give me your arm," she says, and gets a pen out of her backpack.

"Why?" Sean holds his hands behind his back.

"Because I'm going to write my cell number on your arm. If you get lost, just show your arm to someone."

"Mommy, that's weird. I'm not a baby."

"You are not a baby, but you're in a foreign country, and you don't speak the language."

"Who cares? I will be okay," says Sean stubbornly.

Mommy tries to grab his arm, but Sean evades her, and after a short struggle, she gives up.

They walk outside into the sunny stadium.

It's huge! It's the largest stadium in Europe. One hundred-thousand seats are spread out in front of them on three levels of galleries. The tourists stand on the turf where so many famous soccer players have sweated and fought, where some of the most exciting games in the history of soccer have taken place, where Barca has played against Real Madrid, Arsenal, Manchester United, Bayern Munchen, and so many other famous teams.

The visitors disperse across the field, chatting excitedly and taking pictures. Sean touches the turf with awe. He takes his soccer ball from his backpack and starts bouncing it. He executes a short pass to Mommy.

"Mommy, catch!"

Mommy kicks the ball right back to him. Sean receives it and passes it back.

"I'm playing in Camp Nou!" Sean yells as he dribbles.

He imitates a TV commentator's voice: "And the ball goes to Sean, number 10; Sean sees an opening...he passes the defense... he is unstoppable..." he babbles as Mommy takes pictures.

"Let's take a picture of us together." Mommy rummages in her backpack for her selfie stick.

A museum guard approaches them.

"Estan jugando futbol? Estan jugando tiki taka?" he smiles.

Mommy smiles back hesitantly.

"No hablo español...sir."

"I told him I don't speak Spanish," Mommy explains to Sean. "I don't know what he's saying. Good thing I still remember a few words from Spanish class in high school."

"He said we were playing the tiki taka," says Sean confidently.

"Tiki taka?" wonders Mommy.

"Yes. I will explain it to you later. Can you ask him if we can get Messi's autograph?"

"He doesn't know anything about that, Sean."

"Mommy, quickly, before he walks away."

"I don't know how to say it in Spanish."

"Mommy, please. Just try!"

Mommy addresses the guard, uttering each word slowly and clearly.

"Senior... Messi...? Autograph...?"

The guard smiles and replies in Spanish. Mommy smiles back, not understanding a word.

"Messi... autograph?" She tries again, waving her hands in the air as if she is signing something.

"Si, si, Messi." The guard nods approvingly and points at the field. He pats Sean on the head, and walks away.

"I told you. He only works here. It doesn't mean he knows where Messi is," says Mommy.

"You didn't ask him correctly," insists Sean.

"I probably didn't. How did you understand what he said? What's tipi taka?" asks Mommy.

"TIKI TAKA! You really don't know anything about soccer. TIKI TAKA is a style of play that Barca is famous for. It's short passes with movement while maintaining possession of the ball. It's different than traditional formations in soccer, like in a zonal play. Thanks to this tactic, Barcelona has won many matches," Sean recites proudly.

"Oh, really?" Mommy is impressed.

"So how am I going to get Messi's autograph?" demands Sean. Mommy sighs.

"I don't know. I will Google it once we get back to the apartment."

Barcelona Rooftop

Mommy sits on an Oriental-patterned couch in a sunny apartment, her laptop balanced on her knees. Buddha sculptures and candles are scattered on shelves all around her. She types into the search bar: "How to get Messi's autograph."

Boom! A sudden sharp smashing sound jolts her to her feet.

"Sean! What are you doing? Are you playing soccer?" Mommy yells.

She runs outside to the rooftop. Magnificent vistas of Barcelona's old quarter and hilly landscape stretch out in all directions. The famous Sagrada Familia church towers soar up to the sky in all their glory. Every inch of the rooftop is filled with plants and flowerpots.

Sean crouches near an overturned flowerpot, sweeping soil back into the pot with his hands. His soccer ball is next to him on the tiled floor.

"Look what you've done!" Mommy accuses.

"It didn't break."

"Good thing it didn't break. Put everything back the way it was. I told Raul you wouldn't play soccer here. Why can't you ever just listen to me?"

"Mommy, how come Raul lets us stay here?" asks Sean.

"No soccer in the apartment. Do you understand?" Mommy insists.

16

Sean rolls his eyes.

"Answer me, Sean."

"I understand. But how come Raul lets us stay here?" he persists.

"Because we paid him. I'm taking the ball from you," Mommy grabs the ball.

"But we don't know him... How did you find him?" Sean asks.

"On the Internet; there is a special site for people who are renting their homes."

"Really? Is there a site about Messi's home?"

"Probably many," Mommy says.

"Let's go to Messi's home!" Sean cries.

"What are we going to do there? Sit outside and wait until he comes out?" Mommy asks.

"Exactly!" exclaims Sean.

"Honestly, Sean, I'd never think of doing such a thing. We are going to see him at the game. We can try to get an autograph then."

"How?" Sean is not giving up.

"We can stand outside the stadium and watch for the bus with the players. But there will be a crowd and security. Maybe we won't be able to get close," Mommy admits.

Sean considers this.

"Mommy, did you know there's a way we can watch the game without paying?"

"How? You've got me curious."

"There are these little remote-control helicopters with cameras in them. We can send one over to the stadium while the game is going on, and it will broadcast the images back to us."

"Pretty clever, but a completely unrealistic idea," Mommy smiles. "Besides, we don't need a toy helicopter to see the game. We have tickets already."

Mommy turns to walk back into the apartment, the ball under her arm.

"No ball anymore," she says firmly.

"Mommy, you know that Messi does not speak English, don't you?" Sean follows her, watching to see what she will do with the ball.

"If we get to see him, he will understand what we mean if we hand him a pen and paper. But you should not have high expectations," Mommy adds.

She scans the apartment for a good hiding place for the ball.

"I have to have Messi's autograph, please!" cries Sean.

"Oh, Sean, stop nagging. And stop following me around."

"Then let's talk to Daddy. He always has ideas."

Sean approaches the table, grabs Mommy's phone, and dials Daddy on Skype.

The call is connected. They see Daddy sitting in his office.

"Daddy, Mommy says I will not get Messi's autograph," Sean complains.

"Hey, Sean!" Daddy says. "How is Barcelona?"

"Mommy says we won't get to meet Messi."

Mommy slides the ball under the bed quickly.

"You will see him at the game, so that should make you happy," says Daddy.

"But I want his autograph. How can I get it?" Demands Sean.

Daddy considers this for a moment.

"That's more difficult, for sure. First you have to figure out a way to meet him. How would you do that?"

"I told Mommy I want to go to his house," says Sean.

"That's one option. You need to analyze the situation carefully, weigh your options, and make a plan."

"Why are you encouraging him, Daddy? We don't have any options," calls Mommy.

"There are always options." Daddy says, "Write them down orderly on a piece of paper, Sean. Then make a plan."

"I have paper. I will write everything down," beams Sean.

"Once you have plan A, you need to make plan B," adds Daddy.

"What is plan B?" asks Sean.

"Plan A is your best plan. Plan B is the plan to use when plan A doesn't work."

"Okay, I see," says Sean.

"Well, then, I've got to get back to work," Daddy wraps up the conversation.

"Bye, Daddy! Thanks so much!" Sean puts his hand to his lips in a kiss gesture.

"Bye, Daddy! We miss you!" Mommy blows Daddy a kiss as well.

Sean bends down near the bed and reaches for his ball, smiling.

La Sagrada Familia

"Introducing - La Sagrada Familia," Mommy announces as if she is presenting a product on a commercial.

She and Sean are standing in a long line of people, waiting to get tickets to enter a fairy-tale church that defies gravity. Its four towers soar into the clear blue sky, and colorful ornaments of flowers and leaves decorate the details of the magnificent structure.

"No, Mommy! No, Mommy! No, Mommy!" Sean delivers his familiar refrain.

Mommy goes on: "A world heritage site. A masterpiece! A celebrated basilica designed in the Art Nouveau style by the renowned Spanish Architect Gaudi..." she reads from her guide book.

"Mommy, I'm not interested in this church!" interrupts Sean.

"Sean, we are in Barcelona. Who knows when we are going to be here again? You need to get some culture, as well."

"I don't want culture. I only want to do soccer stuff."

Mommy gives him a little nudge forward as the line moves

towards the ticket booth. "Antoni Gaudi was a genius," explains Mommy. "He built many beautiful houses in Barcelona. He had his own unique style. Nobody else ever built houses like his. They are all built in round, organic geometrical forms inspired by nature."

"I'm waiting outside," concludes Sean.

Mommy exhales impatiently.

"If you are going to argue with me, we will go to all of Gaudi's houses in Barcelona! Each and every one of them!" she cries.

"Okay, okay, I will go with you if you want it that much," Sean gives in.

One hour later, Mommy and Sean are inside the Sagrada Familia. They wander in the main hall, maneuvering their way around hordes of tourists, all clicking their cameras and posing for photos near every curved pillar.

"Look at this beautiful colorful mosaic. See how it's made of hundreds of separate pieces?" Mommy points out.

"Mommy, why did you buy those big paper sheets?" Sean asks, spying something in her backpack.

"See the slim supporting pillars? Everyone told Gaudi they wouldn't support the roof, and he proved them wrong. It still stands today, 130 years later."

"What are you going to do with the paper sheets?" insists Sean.

"No one else has been able to build such forms to this day. Gaudi used three-dimensional models when he planned the design. Isn't that super cool?" Mommy tilts her head back and

stares at the lofty dome.

"I can't wait to see Messi in the game on Saturday," says Sean.

Mommy sighs. They continue the tour.

Once they've made it through the tower line, Mommy and Sean head up. The stone staircase is narrow and allows only one person to pass at a time. Windowless hatches along the walls throw patches of light across the steps. From each hatch, they can see the tops of spires, overlaid with colorful mosaics. The tourists pant as they climb slowly up the steep stairs.

"Mommy, this is boring!" announces Sean.

"Why is it boring? It's like a Harry Potter scene!"

"I don't want to climb." Sean halts in place.

"Sean, there are people behind us. You can't stop." Mommy glances at a tourist, who halts his climbing behind Sean, breathing heavily.

Sean folds his arms on his chest and looks at Mommy defiantly.

"Keep climbing, or I will not take you to the game!" Mommy is losing her patience.

"You won't do that." Sean smiles.

"Why stand?" asks the tourist in a Russian accent, motioning upward with his hands.

"I'm sorry." Mommy smiles at him, embarrassed. She turns to Sean.

"Sean, move!" she pleads.

"I want to go shopping in the FC Barcelona official shop," demands Sean.

"Go, no stand!" the tourist says impatiently.

Mommy bends toward Sean, her face a few inches from his, and says in a low tone, "I'm not fooling around. I really don't appreciate the way you are behaving. I organized this whole trip for you. I ask you to do only this one thing for me, and you behave disgracefully. Now please move!"

Mommy turns her back on Sean and resumes climbing.

Sean sulks and goes after her. Mommy and Sean finish the tour without speaking to each other.

Finally, they reach the last hall - the souvenir shop. Book collections, miniature sculptures, cups, toys, and keychains are arranged on glass counters. Sean inspects the merchandise.

"Mommy, buy me a Sagrada Familia keychain," he begs.

"Quiet! Enough is enough!" Mommy calls.

Sean walks angrily to a nearby counter, showing his displeasure and independence. He ignores Mommy, checking out the souvenirs on display.

Mommy is pretending to concentrate on the souvenirs on the counter in front of her, watching Sean from the corner of her eye, grateful that his Barca shirt easily distinguishes him from the other tourists. Sean walks deliberately to a counter on the other end of the hall.

"Excuse me?" A Japanese tourist addresses Mommy.

"Yes?"

"Can you take photo?" The tourist points at herself and her husband, who stands next to her. Mommy agrees, and the husband hands her a sophisticated camera and shows her which button to press.

The couple poses in front of Mommy.

"One moment! Please move," the husband says. He motions with his hands for Mommy to move to the right side so they can get a better picture.

"Ready?" Mommy asks once she is in the new position.

They nod their heads.

Mommy shoots a glance in Sean's direction. She doesn't see him anywhere.

Shocked, she flings the camera at the confused Japanese tourists and runs to the other side of the hall, where Sean was standing.

He is nowhere to be found.

Dumbfounded, she turns around in place, scanning the crowd for Sean's Barca shirt. She feels panic rise in her body. Where is Sean?

She looks for the exits from the hall. One leads toward the church; the other leads out to the street. She runs to the street exit through a short corridor, maneuvering her way through the crowd. She reaches the checkpoint and stands on her toes, trying to get a view of the street above the people's heads.

"Sir, did you see a young boy exit the building just now?" she asks the guard, her words broken with anxiety.

The guard says something in Spanish. Mommy doesn't understand a thing. She runs back inside, loudly calling Sean's name. She reaches the shop and runs between the counters, but there's no sign of Sean. She stops and rummages in her backpack for her phone. Her hands are shaking as she swipes the screen on. Who is she going to call? She throws it back into the backpack and runs off on another round of searches.

Sean comes out of the restroom and into the souvenir shop, satisfied from his little independent adventure. He walks to where Mommy was standing, but he doesn't see her. He sees many people speaking in languages he does not understand. His heart starts pounding in his chest. Where is Mommy? He looks around again and again, but she is nowhere in sight. Tears well up in his eyes. Why did he go to the restroom on his own? He walks around the tourists, looking for Mommy's black coat, but it gets more difficult, as his eyes are filling with more tears. Maybe Mommy left him? Why didn't he listen to her? Why did he upset her?

A lady with a big hat asks him something, but he does not understand what she says. He starts sobbing.

At that moment, Mommy runs into the souvenir shop.

"Mommy!" Sean yells.

"Sean!" Mommy rushes to him, drops to her knees, kissing him and hugging him tightly. They stand locked together for a minute.

"Oh, Sean…you scared me to death." Mommy mumbles as she wipes his tears.

"I didn't see you…I was scared," says Sean.

"Me, too. This can't ever happen again! From now on, we hold

28

hands all the time, okay?"

Sean nods approvingly.

"Good. Where were you?" Mommy asks, still trembling.

"I was right here," mumbles Sean.

"Really? Here?" Mommy wonders, kissing him on his cheek. "Never mind now, the important thing is that we found each other. I have to sit down," she says, and collapses on the floor.

"I have to sit too." Sean joins her.

They sit quietly for a few minutes, passing their water bottle between them, regaining their breath.

"Ready to go?" asks Mommy when she feels somewhat recovered from the experience.

"Yes, Mommy," says Sean, and stands up.

They put their backpacks on their backs. Sean takes a last look at the merchandise.

"Can you buy me a Sagrada Familia statue?" he asks as he gives Mommy his hand.

Mommy gives him a cold look. "Seriously?"

Sean falters. "Ice cream, then?"

Mommy sighs.

"Only if you let me write my phone number on your arm."

The First Team Training

Mommy and Sean, holding hands tightly, walk out of a train station into a small square surrounded by colorful two-story Spanish style houses. Mommy releases her hand from Sean's and gets her phone from her backpack. She checks their location with Google Maps.

"Mommy, what is this place?"

"It's a town outside of Barcelona. The FC Barcelona training stadium is supposed to be here. This is where the first team trains."

"They don't train in Camp Nou?"

"Most of the time, they don't. Or so their site says."

"We are going to see a real training?!" Sean exclaims, thrilled.

"It's a long shot, but we're going to try it." Mommy smiles.

"Let's go!" Sean grabs Mommy's hand and pulls her forward.

They walk and walk, but there is no sign of a building that looks like a famous stadium. Mommy asks people walking by where the FC Barcelona stadium is, but most of them don't speak English. They understand "Barcelona" and "soccer," and they wave their hands in the right direction.

After an hour of walking, they reach the outskirts of the town. They see industrial buildings, dilapidated old houses, and a highway close by. They approach a building complex that stretches for a few blocks, fenced-in as far as the eye can see, with a big FC Barcelona logo on one of the taller buildings.

"That must be it," Mommy says.

Sean grabs her hand and gives her a big smile.

The main gate is closed and there's no one in the security booth, so they take pictures and continue along the sidewalk. Sean lets go of Mommy's hand and runs alongside the wall.

They pass two sporty-looking teenagers with Barcelona Club training uniforms.

"Maybe they are from the youth team," says Sean with admiration.

A maintenance truck is parked along the sidewalk, unloading some goods. There are no more people in sight.

"I don't think there is a training going on now," says Mommy with disappointment.

"Why not?" asks Sean.

"There are too few people around. Or maybe tourists just don't know about this place?"

"We have to find out! Let's go." Sean points forward to where poles with stadium lighting are visible above the wall.

They keep walking. When they turn left at the corner, they see that this side of the wall is lower, about two feet taller than the average man. Above the wall, there is a wire fence covered with a green privacy screen. There is no entrance in sight.

"I'm sorry, my love. I really wanted to see a training, too, but there's no way in. We tried. We did the best we could," says Mommy.

Sean looks at her with disappointment.

"Let's go get something to eat," Mommy sighs.

At that moment, they hear an authoritative voice yell instructions in Spanish from the inside.

"Did you hear that?" asks Sean.

They hear more voices in Spanish.

"I don't understand what they're saying, but it could be a training," says Mommy hopefully.

"Yes! Yes!" shrieks Sean. "They are training inside! Messi! Neymar! Suarez!"

"And we can't get in…" says Mommy.

"Iniesta! Dani Alves! Piqué! Rakitić!" Sean explodes.

"I hear you, Sean."

"And Turan! Bravo! Busquets!" He jumps frantically.

"I get it, Sean, but we still can't get in."

"Look what people wrote here!" Sean points at some writing on the wall.

"Messi - you are number one! - Gary, Hong Kong. Messi is the best - China. Messi - we come from Kurdistan."

"I've got to call Aidan! I've got to tell him! Mommy, give me your phone!" Sean shrieks.

"Aidan is probably at school right now. It's not a good time to call him," Mommy says.

They hear the Spanish voices again.

"Hear that!?" Sean can't control himself. "They are inside!"

Sean pokes his hand into Mommy's backpack and grabs the phone.

"But how do the players understand what the coach says? Neymar is from Brazil. They speak Portuguese in Brazil," observes Mommy.

"Yes, and Rakitić is from Croatia. So what? They all speak Spanish," says Sean confidently as he dials.

"Hello?" Aidan answers the phone.

"Aidan! I'm near the Barca stadium! I'm going to see the Barca team train! I'm going to see Messi!"

"Who cares?" Aidan sneers, "Messi stinks, Ronaldo rules!"

"You don't know anything! I'm hanging up on you!" yells Sean.

"Be nice, Sean. That's not how you speak to friends, or to anybody," Mommy tells him.

Sean throws the phone back into Mommy's backpack.

"So, what's the plan?" he urges.

"I don't know, really," says Mommy.

They inspect the wall. It does have some indentations, and Sean approaches one and tries to fit his foot into it. Mommy looks around to make sure that no one is coming.

"Mommy, I can climb," Sean says.

"I don't think so. The wall is too high… Your toy helicopter would be useful just about now," she smiles.

"Let's go and buy one!" exclaims Sean.

"Sure, let's go! I've got extra cash I need to get rid of!" Mommy jokes.

Sean regards her distrustfully. "It's not funny!"

He turns to the wall and tries to climb it again, but there are no grooves for his hands to hold onto.

"Lift me up, Mommy," he pleads.

"It's still going to be too high, Sean, even if I hold you."

Sean realizes she is right.

"Mommy, the selfie stick! Give it to me," he says.

"Oh…You are brilliant, Sean! It just might stretch far enough to take pictures."

Sean smiles proudly. Mommy gets the selfie stick out of her backpack and stretches it to its maximum length. She connects the cell phone to the stick.

"I'll stick it in my backpack. Once you are up, you'll need to grab it. Let's do it quickly." She looks around nervously.

Mommy puts her hands together. Sean grabs her shoulders and places a foot on her palms. He lifts himself up to a standing position, leaning against the wall with one hand, grabbing Mommy's shoulder with the other.

"Now grab the stick," Mommy says.

Sean balances himself, lets go of her shoulder, and reaches for the selfie stick. He holds it with difficulty, lifting it up as high as he can. It reaches exactly to the bottom of the wire fence.

"Great! Now try to stick it under the screen," Mommy says.

Sean tries a couple of times and finally succeeds.

"It's working! Mommy, it's working!" he shrieks.

"Press the button," Mommy says. "I can't hold you much longer."

Sean tries to adjust his grip on the stick so his finger will reach the button.

"I can't," he says, almost dropping the phone.

"Don't drop my phone!" yells Mommy.

"I'm trying not to," he says, wobbling.

"Señora! Que está haciendo?" an authoritative male voice sounds.

Mommy jolts back in surprise and almost drops Sean. She turns her head to see that a policeman is standing behind them.

"Oh, hello." Mommy smiles nervously at him and lowers Sean down. Sean loses his grip on the selfie stick, and it falls on the asphalt.

"Qué está haciendo?" asks the policeman in a grave voice.

"No hablo español, sir." Mommy picks up her phone, quickly glancing at the screen to see if it's still working.

"De donde erán?" the policeman asks. "Son turistas?"

"Yes, tourists." Mommy falters. "I don't speak Spanish." She flashes him a friendly smile.

"No go inside," says the policeman sternly.

"We were not trying to go inside...we only wanted to see..."

explains Mommy anxiously.

"Dáme sus pasaportes, por favor," the policeman says.

Mommy understands the word "passports."

"I don't understand what you're saying, sir," she says.

"Give passports!" the policeman demands in a louder voice.

"Oh, passports?" Mommy asks dreadfully.

"Si! Passports!"

Mommy's mind races. What does he want their passports for? Can he hold them? She fumbles in her backpack, trying to buy time.

The policeman looks at them impatiently and taps his foot.

"Is he going to arrest us?" asks Sean, frightened.

"I don't know," mumbles Mommy.

"Why?" Sean panics. He moves closer to Mommy and grabs her shirt.

"PASSPORTS, madam!" the policeman loses his patience.

"I'm looking...sir..." Mommy searches her backpack frantically.

Tears start running down Sean's cheeks. Mommy stops searching and pats him on the shoulder.

"Don't cry, Seany. Don't be afraid," she murmurs, glancing at the policeman.

Sean cries harder.

"My son didn't mean any harm, sir," pleads Mommy. "Can't we just go?"

The policeman looks confused.

"No se entiendo," he says.

"Can we go? Please?" Mommy waves her hands to demonstrate

a departure and joins her palms together in a pleading gesture.

Mommy and Sean look at the policeman expectantly. The policeman falters.

"Okay, señora," he says.

"Thank you! Thank you very much!" Mommy gives the policeman a grateful bow.

She grabs Sean by the hand and walks him away quickly, not looking back.

"He is not going to arrest us?" Sean wipes his face.

"You were great, Sean! You saved us. Good job!" says Mommy with relief.

"Was the policeman going to take us to jail, Mommy?"

"I don't think so. Let's just get out of here."

They glance back at the policeman, who walks away in the other direction. Sean gets a marker from his backpack and quickly scribbles on the wall, "Sean was here!"

Super Creative Brain Power Juice

The La Boqueria market is packed. Locals and tourists walk among the stands of fruit and vegetables piled in colorful arrangements. Vendors yell to advertise their merchandise. Mommy and Sean sit at the bar of a food stand between other tourists. A chalkboard displays the daily menu. Inside the service area, a big guy in a white chef's jacket is grilling seafood on a griddle. A plate with fish, grilled vegetables, and the famous Spanish ceviche dish sits in front of Mommy and Sean.

"I want a hamburger and chips!" complains Sean.

"No, today we eat healthy. You need to get some good protein in you if you want to be a professional soccer player someday," says Mommy.

"This is disgusting!"

"Messi eats this," protests Mommy.

"I don't believe you."

Mommy sighs.

40

"So, were you scared of the policeman?" she distracts Sean as she shoves a fork full of fish into his mouth.

"Not really." Sean takes the bite.

"I was," admits Mommy, and succeeds in placing another piece of fish into Sean's mouth.

"What now?" asks Sean while chewing.

"Now we rest. I've had enough for one day," Mommy says. "The game is tomorrow. We should take it easy."

"Yes, The Clasico! Barca is going to destroy Real Madrid! Ronaldo is history!" Sean exclaims.

"Why do you call it The Clasico?" asks Mommy.

"That's what a game between Barcelona and Real Madrid is called. The Real Madrid team is Barcelona's biggest rival."

"I'm worried. It's going to be packed and crazy out there," Mommy says.

"Barca didn't lose once in 39 games! They have a ten-point lead on Real. Even if Real wins, they don't have a chance to win La Liga," Sean tells her.

"Listen to me, Sean, you will have to stay close to me. And in case you get lost, you need to show someone your arm with the phone number. Okay?" Mommy rolls his sleeve up to check that the number is still there.

"And what about Messi's autograph?"

"Answer me, please. Say okay."

"Okay. What about the autograph?"

"I don't know. Drink this juice." Mommy moves a glass of

orange-carrot juice in front of Sean.

"I want a soda."

"We will arrive early and try to see the players as they come in. Maybe we will get close enough to ask for an autograph." Mommy sticks the juice right in Sean's face.

"That's your plan?" asks Sean.

"Do you have a better one?" Mommy inquires.

"Not right now," admits Sean.

"Drink the juice. Its super creative brain power juice with extra vitamins. It can help you get ideas."

Sean takes a thoughtful sip of the juice.

Game Day

An excited crowd huddles around the barrier on both sides of the entrance road to the Camp Nou stadium. Squeezed in the front, cell phone camera ready in hand, Mommy and Sean are intently observing every passing car. Fancy cars drive by, but so far, there have been no famous soccer players behind any of the dark windows. Sean runs a hand through his hair, checking that his hairdo is still in place. Stripes are painted on his and Mommy's cheeks in red, yellow, and blue - the FC Barcelona colors. Sean has his Barca scarf and clothes on. A large roll of paper sticks out of Mommy's backpack.

"When is Messi coming?" asks Sean.

"Two hours till the game...I think it shouldn't be long now," Mommy answers.

Another car enters the driveway. A security guard stops it and asks the driver for papers.

"When is Messi coming?" Mommy yells to him as the car pulls away.

"Messi is already inside," the guard smiles.

There is a collective sigh of disappointment all around, and the crowd disperses in the direction of the stadium.

Forty-five minutes before the game, the gates open. The excited crowd moves to the stadium entrance doors. Fans from all over the world chat in Spanish, French, Italian, Arabic, English, German, Turkish, Japanese, and other languages. Many wear clothes with the Barcelona colors and symbols. Some have their faces painted,

45

too. Sean holds Mommy's hand tightly.

They stand in the line for the security check. When they get to the checkpoint, the security guard points at the large roll of paper in Mommy's bag, shaking her head in disapproval, saying something in Spanish. Mommy rolls open the poster, made from the paper she bought. It says "We love you, Messi! Go, Barca!" in English.

The guard points to the trash can.

"Why? It's just a poster. I made it myself," questions Mommy.

The guard keeps pointing at the trash. Mommy sees that the people behind them are starting to get restless. She gives up and dumps the poster.

It is a while before Mommy and Sean find their places. They wander in awe among the excited fans, until they find their seats in the second gallery in the center of the field. The stadium is packed. Music is playing. People are taking pictures of themselves with the famous soccer field in the background.

The Barca hymn begins playing, and everybody sings along. When it ends, the Barca team players start coming out one by one from the pitch. The announcer presents each player by name.

"Neymar Junior!" he yells, and the crowd goes, "Ney-mar, Ney-mar!"

"Gerard Piqué!"

"Piiii-qué!" the crowd repeats.

"Leo Mmmme----ssi!"

Everybody in the crowd goes out of their minds, including Sean, who can't contain his excitement over finally seeing his hero in real life!

When the Real Madrid team comes out onto the field, the Barca fans stand up, shout their lungs out, and whistle in contempt. Especially when Ronaldo, Madrid's captain, runs in.

"Boo! Boo!" Sean joins in.

"That's not nice," says Mommy.

"Boo!" Sean smiles and yells louder.

Across the stadium, the Real Madrid fans yell, too, to cheer on their team, attempting to be louder than the Barca fans.

The soccer players start their warmup. Messi and Neymar are passing a ball between them. Messi's calculated precise movements and Neymar's agile style can be clearly distinguished.

excited, Sean?" Mommy asks her son, who watches _ntly.

"Don't talk to me right now, Mommy. I'm concentrating," he replies without turning his head.

The whistle is blown, and the game kicks off. The Barca team plays in their usual style of short passes as they move towards the opposing goal, looking for opportunities. Their attacking trio, Messi-Neymar-Suarez, searches for openings.

Real Madrid plays a defensive tactic. They are creating a strong formation around their goal, each player guarding a Barca player tightly, not giving them any chances. Real's famous forwards, Ronaldo, Gareth, and Benzema, try attack tactics and tricks of their own.

The pressure is immense. Both teams are playing very aggressively. Fouls are committed on both sides as they struggle for the possession of the ball. With each foul, the crowd gets to their feet and yells in discontent.

Ramos, an aggressive Real Madrid player, fouls Messi. Messi falls face down on the turf, but the referee does not call it.

"What? Why?" yells Sean.

Though the Barcelona team holds the ball for most of the time, they fail to score. The first half of the game ends 0-0.

At halftime, Mommy and Sean go to get popcorn, holding hands tightly.

Then the second half starts.

At the sixtieth minute, Barca attacks. Raketich's corner kick is

met brilliantly by the defender Piqué, who downs a stunning header into the goal. Camp Nou explodes! 1-0 to Barcelona!

"Yes! Go Barca!" yells Sean.

On the field, the struggle goes on, though with less pressure from Barca, who feels more confident now. They don't need more than 1-0 to win over their rival.

At seventy-two minutes on the clock, Real snatches the ball from Barca and forms a counter attack. They advance to the Barca side of the field before Barca's defense is ready, and Benzema scores a goal with an acrobatic scissor kick. The score is 1-1!

"Oh, my gosh!" wails Mommy.

Sean is speechless.

The game continues and Real Madrid plays more confidently. Suddenly, every time they attack, they look dangerous. The Barca fans hold their breath. Sean bites his fingernails.

Though the score is still 1-1, it looks like Barcelona has gone to pieces. The sturdy Real defense doesn't let them close to their goal.

In another attack by Real, from the left flank, Gareth passes the ball to Ronaldo. Ronaldo stops the ball with his chest and shoots it into the net. Beautiful goal!

Real Madrid fans yell at the top of their lungs. Ronaldo performs his signature goal celebration.

Mommy holds her hands to her face. Sean can't believe his eyes.

What a disaster! Real Madrid came from behind and took the

lead, only ten minutes before the game's end!

Barca struggles on, but nothing seems to work. All their attacks get blocked, and Real Madrid is stalling for time. The game ends with a defeat for Barcelona, 2-1 for Real.

Mommy and Sean sit speechless in their chairs. Tears well up in Sean's eyes.

"How can it be? How can Messi lose?" mumbles Sean.

"Everybody loses sometimes," Mommy says sadly.

"No, not Messi!" cries Sean.

"But he always pulls himself together, learns from his mistakes, and continues," Mommy consoles herself and Sean.

Finally, the shocked Barca fans begin to disperse.

Messi's House

It is a sleepy Sunday morning in a beachfront Spanish town. The train from Barcelona stops at the two-track train station, and several people get off. Mommy and Sean are among them. They walk out into the town's main square. Mommy looks around, shielding her eyes from the sun. She sees a playground with a few sculptures, some Turkish restaurants, and mountains in the distance. She checks her phone and leads the way.

"How do you know where Messi lives?" asks Sean.

"I looked it up on the Internet. According to Google Maps, we have about half an hour of walking to do."

They walk along the main street in the direction of the green hills. They pass by a patisserie with chocolate sculptures of Messi in the display window.

As they move away from the city center, there are fewer shops and more residential houses. When they reach the foot of the hills, the three-story houses become private homes with well-kept gardens in front of them. Here and there, there's a pleasant smell of charcoal burning, as people are getting started with their Sunday barbecues.

The road gets steeper as it curves up the hills. Villas replace the houses, many with expansive terraces and dazzling views of the Mediterranean Sea. On the top of the hill, Mommy and Sean find themselves in a natural forest, with fancy villas nestled among the pine and oak trees.

"Mommy, are you sure that we are going the right direction?" asks Sean.

"I think so. There is no one around to ask," Mommy answers.

Finally, they reach the address Mommy found on the internet.

"That's it, Sean! That's Messi's house," Mommy says excitedly.

"Wow! I'm near Messi's house!" Sean yelps, and takes her phone, snapping pictures of the house from every possible angle.

Since it's built higher on a slope, the modest house is clearly visible from the road. On the balcony of the neighboring house, an elderly couple is drinking coffee in the sun, talking in Spanish. There are no houses further down the road, just the forest.

"Mommy, do you think Messi is at home?" asks Sean.

"It's Sunday. He might be at home, recuperating from last night's defeat. But this doesn't look right," Mommy adds.

"What do you mean?"

"The house is too visible, too old. Maybe it's not Messi's house."

"It's not? Are you sure? Ask the couple on the balcony," suggests Sean.

Mommy hesitates.

"Excuse me!" she yells finally, interrupting the quiet Sunday morning and the gentle chirping of the birds. "Donde casa Messi, por favor?"

The couple stares down at her and at Sean.

"Messi casa?" Mommy gives it another shot.

The man gives her a long explanation in Spanish, from which Mommy deducts that they need to go to the other side of the hill, in the direction the man points with his finger.

"Gracias!" Mommy thanks him and they walk on.

They reach the other side of the hill. Lavish properties follow the curve of the road between the thick trees.

"We need to find someone who speaks English. I don't know where we're going," says Mommy.

They keep wandering in the neighborhood until they stumble upon a couple in their forties, walking their husky dog.

"Excuse me? Do you speak English? Do you know where Messi's house is?" Mommy tries.

The couple laughs. Then the man answers Mommy in broken English. He knows where Messi lives. It's a big white villa with a tall white wall around it. It's impossible to see anything inside. The man explains how they can reach it, but he sees that Mommy is still confused. He takes out his phone and shows her the exact location on Google Maps.

Sean and Mommy start panting as they march up the hill again.

"When will we get there?" Sean whines.

Mommy is irritated.

"Have I been here before? How should I know?"

"Because you are Mommy," Sean replies. "Mommy knows everything."

Mommy laughs.

"I don't know everything. Nobody knows everything," she says.

They reach the street the man showed them on the map. There is no one around. They find a tall white concrete wall with security cameras and no view of the inside.

Mommy pauses and stares at the metal gate with the house number on it.

"Are you sure that's it?" asks Sean.

"I'm pretty sure. Looks much more like it. The address I found on the Internet must have been wrong."

"But I can't see anything. The wall is too tall," says Sean.

"It makes sense. Messi needs his privacy. Otherwise, he would be bothered constantly by fans."

"Lift me up, Mommy."

"No way! You want us to get in trouble again?"

"Let's take pictures, then," Sean offers.

Mommy takes a few pictures of Sean standing in front of the gate.

"What do we do now? How do we get an autograph?" asks Sean once they're done.

"We can only wait. Maybe Messi will come out."

Mommy takes a poster out of her backpack and rolls it open.

"What's that?" Sean asks.

"I made another poster," explains Mommy proudly.

Sean looks at the colorful text and a drawing of a plane and a heart.

"What does it say?" he asks.

"It's in Spanish. It says: Messi, we flew from far away to see you. Please give us an autograph. We love you."

"I thought you didn't know Spanish?" wonders Sean.

"I Googled it."

"It's lame!" Sean declares.

"Here, hold it." Mommy hands him the poster.

"You hold it," he protests.

"Why me? It's more meaningful in the hands of a little boy," Mommy points out.

Sean holds the poster reluctantly.

After a minute he passes Mommy the poster and grabs her phone. He sets it to video mode and hits record.

"Hello, friends," Sean imitates a host on a TV show. "Today, I will show you Messi's house!" He films the gate with the house number, then continues along the wall. "In case you didn't know, Messi is the best soccer player in the world. He is..."

At that moment, the gate opens, and a tall security guard in a blue uniform comes out.

Sean freezes. Mommy smiles at the guard nervously.

The security guard regards them suspiciously and angrily addresses Mommy in Spanish, while pointing at Sean.

"No photos?" Mommy guesses.

"Mommy, is he going to arrest me?" Sean asks fearfully.

"No, but stop filming. Put the phone down," Mommy says.

"No photo," the guard says.

He notices their poster, but doesn't find it amusing. He tells Mommy they need to leave. Mommy understands this from his irritated tone and his hand movements.

"We're going, we're going," she assures him as she rolls up the poster.

"Come on, Sean, we need to go," she says.

"But I didn't get an autograph from Messi!" Sean reminds her.

"The guard doesn't want us here," Mommy urges.

Standing with folded arms, the guard waits for them to leave.

Suddenly, a Mastiff dog runs out of the open gate, wagging its tail, happy to be free. The guard curses in panic and rushes to catch it.

"Mommy, it's Messi's dog!" Sean exclaims. "I saw photos of it on the Internet!"

"Cool!" says Mommy.

With little smiles on their faces, they watch the guard as he runs after the dog and struggles to get a hold of it.

Finally, the guard catches the pooch and carries it, wriggling in his arms, into the house. He gives Mommy and Sean a last look to make sure they are leaving. Mommy puts her backpack on her back and throws the poster into a trash bin nearby.

The guard closes the gate.

"Sean, we did our best. We tried everything. It's time to go."

"But, Mommy! We can't give up now!"

"You want to get in trouble? We need to move it!" Mommy turns to walk away.

Sean follows her reluctantly. After a few steps, he reaches into his backpack and pulls out a small package. He runs back to the wall and flings the package over it as hard as he can.

"Plan B!" he yells as he throws.

"What did you do? Are you crazy?" Mommy cries out.

"It's a package for Messi."

"You can't just throw stuff into people's homes!" yells Mommy.

The dog starts barking furiously behind the wall. Mommy and Sean look at each other fearfully. They hear angry Spanish voices getting closer.

"Oh, my gosh, Sean, we've got to get out of here!"

The outraged voices approach the gate.

"Run!" Mommy grabs Sean's hand and pulls him along with her as she darts away. They run as fast as they can. Behind them, they hear the gate open.

"Faster!" yells Mommy.

They turn a corner onto another street, not looking back. The dog's barking is getting closer.

"Faster!"

Out of breath, backpacks pounding on their backs, they race down the street, holding hands tightly.

"I love you, Mommy!" yells Sean. "You are the best mommy in the world!"

Autograph

It is nighttime at the Barcelona airport. Mommy and Sean are slouched on adjacent seats by their gate, waiting for their flight home. They are both very tired.

"Sean, try to get some sleep," suggests Mommy.

"I can't sleep, Mommy. Let's do a night talk."

"I'm exhausted." Mommy shifts in place, trying to find a more comfortable position.

"Parents should have night talks with their kids. They taught us that at school," Sean says.

"What's a night talk, anyway?" Mommy is curious.

"You have to answer three of my questions," he explains.

"Three questions? Can we make it just one question today?"

"Okay," agrees Sean.

"Can I ask you a question? I have one too," offers Mommy.

"What's your question?"

"What was in the package you gave Messi?"

"My Messi scrapbook," Sean replies proudly.

"Your scrapbook?" Mommy is startled. "The one you've been working on for years? With all the best Messi pictures? And the poems you wrote about him?"

"Yes, I wanted to give him my most precious thing."

"Wow! I'm glad you consider it your most precious thing. And I'm sure Messi appreciates it, too." Mommy laughs and gives Sean a little hug.

"Can I ask my question now?" says Sean.

"Go ahead,"

"What is Messi's haircut called?" asks Sean.

"Messi's haircut?!" Mommy laughs.

Just then, a commotion begins near the next gate. A group of soccer players in white uniforms walks by, and an excited crowd forms around them. Sean jumps up.

"Mommy, it's the Real Madrid team!"

"Real Madrid!?!"

"Yes! Yes! It's Ronaldo!" yells Sean.

"Ronaldo?"

"The third guy back. With the terrible hair!" Sean exclaims.

"Oh, my gosh! Sean - run and get an autograph!"

"No way! Ronaldo is no Messi!" cries Sean.

The group of soccer players slows down as a crowd clusters around them, asking them for autographs.

"They must be going home after the game," says Mommy. "Too bad Aidan isn't here! Sean, get an autograph for Aidan!"

"No way! I deleted him from my friends list."

"You did not! Do it for him! He'd be flipping out!" Mommy urges.

"I also deleted him from the group 'Best and coolest soccer players of 3rd grade'," Sean goes on.

"Come on! That's not how you treat friends!" Mommy fumbles in her backpack and hands Sean paper and a pen. "Quickly! Go! Before they're gone!"

With a sigh, Sean runs hesitantly toward the group of soccer players and stands in line with the other fans.

As he waits, and stares at the second best soccer player in the world, Sean smiles. Aidan is really going to owe him one! And although this vacation might not have turned out quite the way he expected, it's sure been a lot of fun. Besides, there is still hope for plan B, since he enclosed with the package to Messi an autograph request and his home address.

Two months later this arrives in the mail:

Dear Sean,

You will have a successful soccer career if your kick is as strong as your arm.

Leo Messi

END OF BOOK 2

To be continued...

To check out the other books
in the series and get notified when
the next book is coming visit:
sean-wants-to-be-messi.com

74100317R00042

Made in the USA
Middletown, DE
19 May 2018